A Wi

Cleaner's

Nightmare

Anthony

John

O'Rourke

Wilf Beaton

Introduction.

This is the story of how a window cleaner who was new to his job got caught up in trouble that not many people would have imagined.

Wilf Beaton was a bachelor who lived in Salford and had done a few ordinary jobs during his time to make a living.

When he was 40 years of age he decided to open his own business as a Window Cleaner but he ran into problems that he did not anticipate.

Find out about how he dealt with the situation in this easy-to-read account of an extraordinary fortnight in the life of a window cleaner.

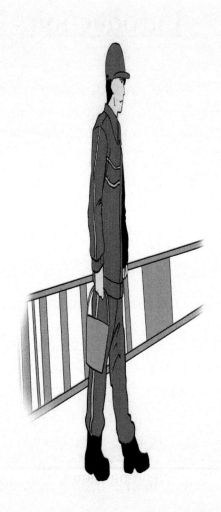

List of Addresses.

4 Vineyard Street. Wilf's address.

Moorgate Lane. On the window cleaning round.

Kings Drive. On the window cleaning round.

Queens Road. On the window cleaning round.

Duke Lane. On the window cleaning round.

Regent Drive. On the window cleaning round.

Royal Street. On the window cleaning round.

Court Road. On the window cleaning round.

Lawyers Lane. On the window cleaning round.

Jury Close. On the window cleaning round.

List of Characters. (who speak in the book)

Wilf Beaton Window Cleaner.

Dave Preston former owner of the business.

A resident of 25 Moorgate Lane, Salford.

Don Wilf's friend at the Grove.

Terry Wilf's friend at the Grove.

Dale Wilf's friend at the Grove.

Rick Wilf's friend at the Grove.

A Chinese man dressed like Bruce Lee Works at the local Take Away.

Mr. Collins Dentist on Kings Avenue.

Young Mother Outside the Grove Pub.

Associates In the street.

Mrs. Grennelly Resident of 17 Queens Road.

Mr. Evans. Estate Agent Manager on Duke Lane.

Detective Inspector Reeves Greater Manchester Police.

Detective Constable Hilton Greater Manchester Police.

Policeman in the Police Car Greater Manchester Police.

Freda Jenkins Landlady of the Grove.

P.C.Morgan Greater Manchester Police.

P.C.Brown Greater Manchester Police.

Mick Jenkins Landlord of the Grove.

Chapter One.

Wilf Beaton was a well-known character in the vicinity. Wilf was born in Salford in 1930. He was evacuated to Bangor, North Wales during the war with his brother William who was six years his senior. A couple from the town called Mr. and Mrs. Jones looked after them and they were educated at the local school.

His mother died of cancer in 1942 and his Father died on D-Day invading the beaches of Normandy. That just left William and himself as his Grandparents on both sides had passed away long before William and Wilf were born and their parents were the only ones in their families. They kept in touch with Mr. and Mrs. Jones at Christmas with a card but never returned there.

William bought a flat outright at 4 Vineyard Street in Salford when the war ended in 1945 as his Father had left a house to William and himself which they sold. Sadly, William lost his life in a car accident in 1948, and Wilf was left as the only surviving Beaton at the age of 18. He knew he may have had some distant relatives but had lost touch with them. After the war, he did his National Service with the R.A.F. He trained in Britain and did service for the country. When he had completed his two years of conscription, he moved back to the flat and got a job in a warehouse that supplied health foods to different wholesalers all over the country.

He worked at the warehouse until 1960 and the company then relocated to the south of the country. Wilf was not interested in moving and got another job as a warehouseman for a local food company. Again he stayed on the shop floor as he was not interested in taking on a foreman or supervisor's position as he was quite content to do a job without too much responsibility.

He worked on the shop floor for another decade ordering supplies and taking orders for local schools and hospitals. During his leisure time, Wilf would go to Manchester. During mid-week after work, he would go shopping in the local town and buy the essentials for a bachelor. On Tuesday and Friday evenings he used to visit the local pub called 'The Grove.' He was a regular in the place and the bar staff liked him.

In November 1971 he got made redundant as his employers closed part of the premises down. He took a break from work. He had not been away over the years and decided to go back to North Wales on a visit. Mr. and Mrs. Jones had died in the 1950s and he caught the train and stayed at a bed and breakfast in the town where he spent the war years when he was growing up with William. It brought back some fond memories. The trip did him good as it recharged his batteries and he spent most of the days walking by the sea visiting a few bars and reuniting with a few people who were still there and remembered him. He returned to his flat and spent some of his time there and some of the time visiting Manchester buying a few things and doing some window shopping.

He wondered what he would do next and after a few weeks was looking through the local newspaper where he saw an advert.

WINDOW CLEANING ROUND FOR SALE. GOOD BUSINESS. GREAT POTENTIAL.

GENUINE REASON FOR SALE:

OWNER RETIRING AFTER 15 YEARS.

APPLY IN PERSON TO:

Mr. Dave Preston, 25 Moorgate Lane, Salford.

After reading the advert Wilf sat down with a cup of tea and thought about the position. 'Hmm, Window Cleaning.' he said to himself. He thought I have cleaned the windows at the warehouse and the factory over the years and found it alright.

The next day he walked down to 25 Moorgate Lane. It was an old house with a big red door. He knocked and waited. Then a tall, slim man answered.

'Hello' said Wilf. 'I have come about the Window Cleaning Business.'

'Are you Dave Preston?'

'Yes.' he replied. 'Come in and I will tell you about it.'

Wilf then entered the house and sat in the Living Room with Dave.

Even though they had never met before they had a very friendly conversation. Dave told Wilf about the business and how he could make a living out of it if he worked hard and kept the customers happy. Dave was retiring to Cornwall later in the year and the business had served him alright. He was also a Truck Driver and did that at the weekend to supplement his income.

After a long conversation, Wilf and Dave agreed that they would work together the following week and see if he liked the job and felt suited to it. If he wanted to take over the business they would discuss what it would cost and hopefully come to an arrangement about when he would take over. They agreed to meet at the same place at 9.00 am. the following Monday morning.

Chapter Two.

During the weekend Wilf did his usual thing. He went shopping at the local supermarket. He used to always go to the same place on Fridays as that was his payday. He used to stock up for the whole week and enjoyed cooking and cleaning his flat at the weekend.

On Friday evening he got changed into his smart casual clothes and took his usual walk down to the Grove. He sat in his usual place and waited for the regulars to come in. At about 7.30 pm. Don and Terry arrived. They walked in and said'

'Evening, Wilf, how are you?'

Wilf replied 'Alright thanks!'

The three men then sat together and Wilf started to tell them about his possible change of career. At about 8.00 pm. his other friends Dale and Rick arrived and he informed them about it also.

'Interesting that Wilf.' said Rick.

'If it works you could be the best window cleaner in the area.' he added.

'Your business might grow and you may start employing people' said Dale.

'Yeah! Beaton's Window Cleaning Service.' said Don.

Wilf laughed and replied, ' I won't be a window cleaner, I will be known as a transparent wall technician.'

The regulars spent the usual evening talking about what they had done during the week. They had all been busy at work and Dale and Rick were married with families to look after. They still found time to come out on

Tuesday and Friday evenings and it was quite a regular meeting point for everyone after a working week.

Dale had been working as an engineer and Rick installed central heating. They met on Tuesday evenings at night school for guitar-playing lessons and then would come to the Grove later after class.

Wilf sometimes met them there and sometimes they would play a few tunes and sing. It was a great way to entertain the locals as they enjoyed the sing-a-long too.

They had been friends for many years and had met at the same venue most of the time.

Wilf would often tell stories about how he bought Fish and Chips from the local takeaway on his way home and went back the following evening as when he arrived back at his home, the fish was not cooked properly.

One evening he stated that he went back to the takeaway the night after he bought fish and chips and said to the Chinese gentleman behind the counter,

'Excuse me, I bought fish and chips from here last night and the quality of the fish was terrible. When I got home the batter peeled off in the wrapping paper and it was horrible.'

He then explained how the Chinese man had a discussion with somebody in the back of the shop and a man ran out from the back dressed like Bruce Lee.

He said, 'What's the problem?'

Wilf replied, 'Excuse me, I bought fish and chips from here last night and the quality of the fish was terrible.'

The man dressed like Bruce Lee said,

'You come back here tonight!!! We give you good deal!!!'

However, Wilf did not return. He also thought that the suet puddings in shops today were gruesome.

'These puddings they give you in the shop today. They are like grenades aren't they?'

'You look for the pin on them!' everyone laughed.

He also stated,

'Fish in the past used to be excellent it was cooked well, lovely and crisp.'

'Well.' stated Dale 'things aren't as good as they used to be are they?'

Everyone agreed that that was the way things went. Still, on most Friday evenings they found time to go to the takeaway after their pints of beer followed by a couple of shorts. They all lived near the pub and walked home quietly.

Chapter Three.

The usual weekend passed and Wilf got up early on Monday morning ready to start his new employment. He put on a pair of overalls and a hat as it was a cold winter's morning. He walked out of his flat on Vineyard Street and down to Moorgate Lane. It was about a ten-minute walk. He thought about the day ahead and if he would be suited to the work.

He knocked at Dave Preston's door at 9.00 am. and Dave answered,

'Morning Wilf, ready for the day?' said Dave.

'Yes, as ready as I can be.' replied Wilf.

They then set off with buckets, leathers, detergent, and a ladder and walked down to Kings Drive to start the day's work.

Kings Drive was full of shops and houses and Dave served a few of the places on it. Dave set up the ladders at Mr. Collins who was the local Dentist.

'This is how you set up for an upstairs Wilf' said Dave.

'You place the ladders at the bottom window and raise them so as you can go upstairs. What do you want to do? Do you want to try it now or do you want to watch me first?'

Wilf replied ' I will have a go myself and can you watch me please?'

'Sure.' said Dave.

Wilf climbed the ladder with his bucket and equipment. He made it to the top and looked down. He then started to clean the windows with his leathers and sponges.

'Good Wilf.' said Dave. 'You are taking to this like a duck to water.'

Wilf started making faces through the window. He was making expressions as if he was having his teeth pulled out.

Suddenly, Mr. Collins appeared at the bottom of the ladder.

' Hey, you stop messing about.' he shouted.

'What's wrong.' said Dave.

'Your mate. One of the patients was having his filling done and saw him through the window making painful expressions. It is not funny.' said Mr. Collins.

Dave started laughing and Wilf came down the ladder.

'Sorry' said Wilf. 'It was only a practical joke.'

'Don't go playing stupid practical jokes like that when a nervous patient is having his teeth seen to or another window cleaner can do my windows.' said the Dentist.

'Listen' said Dave. 'He is new to the job and did not mean any harm.'

'We are sorry aren't we Wilf?'

'What, of course.' said Wilf. 'It won't happen again.'

'To right, it won't' said Mr. Collins.

He then walked back up the stairs to his surgery shaking his head.

Dave then said to Wilf, 'That's a good start for your first customer!'

'I know' said Wilf. 'Some people don't have the same sense of humour do they?'

Dave and Wilf realized that this was a bit of fun but the dentist didn't. Still, that was their first point of call. A few customers were on Kings Drive and they worked well together. Wilf seemed to be picking the job up very well. He enjoyed leathering and washing the windows with his leathers, sponges, and drying cloths.

The dentist was the initial place and they then did a restaurant, a news agency, an estate agent, and some houses on the Drive. When they had finished the job they picked up their money at each place.

The day's work seemed to go well and Wilf was picking things up quickly and easily. He remembered the times when he cleaned the windows in the warehouse and put this to good use. They completed about 10 places during the first day and Wilf and Dave split the money between them. They did not stop for lunch just worked straight through and they finished working in the early evening. They looked quite a sight Dave a tall, slim guy, and Wilf and medium build man with buckets, leathers, and ladders. Wilf looked quite a character in his overalls.

When they finished they carried all the equipment back to a lock-up garage on Moorgate Lane not far from Dave's house.

As they were putting the things back Dave turned to Wilf and asked,

'Well, how do you feel Wilf?' 'Did you like the work?'

'Yes, it was alright even with the first customer who was a bit serious it was alright.'

'Great.' said Dave.

'Shall we meet tomorrow morning at my house again at 9.00 a.m. and we can do another street. I think you are finding your feet with the job and if we continue we can have a chat very soon about the business.'

'

Sure.' replied Wilf. 'See you tomorrow, have a good evening, Dave.'

'You too, Wilf, see you tomorrow.'

Chapter Four.

The next morning Wilf got up made himself a bit of breakfast and got ready for work. Wilf was thinking about the job and although he felt quite suited to the work the only thing that concerned him was working outside. It was winter now and the days were short and cold and he would have to do a lot of work in a short amount of time. Like everyone he wasn't getting any younger so he wondered about how long he could do the job for if he was to take the business on.

The other factor that was playing on his mind was the business. He thought about how much Dave would want to sell the window cleaning round to him. He didn't think that Dave would accept a weekly commission because he was retiring to Cornwall and they of course would not see each other then. Still, he put this to the back of his mind for the time being and concentrated on what was going on now.

'Morning Wilf.'

'Morning Dave.' 'Where are we working today?'

'Queens Road.' replied Dave.

They then walked from Moorgate Lane to Queens Road which was about a five-minute walk. If there was a very positive thing about the business it was that Dave served 9 or 10 streets that were all within walking distance of his house and lock up garage. Dave had not used a car as each street was near his house so this cut out the overheads of petrol, car insurance, maintenance, etc. This was very important for Wilf as he never learned how to drive and wasn't interested in owning a car.

The ladders were lightweight designed and expensive as they were new on the market so they were very light and easy to carry although it was a bit awkward when they came to turning corners in narrow streets. They would get some water from their customers and bring a container to fill up if they needed fresh water. The day started again and Dave watched Wilf clean most of the houses on Queens Road. This area was all residential so they were cleaning the windows of houses.

Dave put up the ladders at number 3 and Wilf once again climbed up.

Wilf started singing,

'Now I go cleaning windows to earn an honest bob for a nosy parker it's an interesting job.'

Dave started laughing,

'Hey, Wilf don't go saying that you'll get us into trouble again like you did with Mr. Collins yesterday.'

Wilf laughed and said,

'Well, it's crazy but true.'

They laughed and carried on with the work. They did most of the houses on Queens Road and once again collected the money. When they finished, they shared it again. They knocked at the door first to see if anyone was in and if nobody was Dave had some notes printed saying.

WINDOW CLEANER CALLED.

WE WILL CALL BACK WITHIN 14 DAYS. ANY PROBLEMS PLEASE CONTACT:

DAVE PRESTON AT 25 MOORGATE LANE.

It was a cool day but the sun was shining and they got on with the work again. They finished at about 4.00 pm. and carried the equipment back to the lock-up garage.

When they had done this Dave said to Wilf,

'Do you like the work, Wilf?'

Wilf replied, 'Yes, I think I can do it, but I would like to take a few days to think about it first.'

'Sure.' Dave said. 'Why don't you come around on Saturday when you have had a chance to think things over and I will be at home all day.'

'Great' said Wilf. 'See you on Saturday at 12 midday.'

'Yes, that's fine, I will talk to you then.' 'Before you go here is a list of the streets and roads that I have on the round.' 'Have a look at it and let me know if there is anywhere you don't know but I think you will as there are only ten streets and they are all walking distance from here.' 'It's only a small business.'

'Thanks, Dave.' 'I'll have a look and then talk to you about it on Saturday. Bye!'

'Bye, Wilf see you soon.'

Wilf then walked back to Vineyard Street. He got home and started making some dinner. He thought about the job and looked at the list Dave had given him. It read

10 houses on Moorgate Lane.

5 Businesses and 5 Houses on Kings Drive.

10 houses on Queens Road.

5 Businesses and 5 houses on Duke Lane.

7 houses on Regent Drive.

7 houses on Royal Street.

8 houses on Court Road.

6 houses on Lawyers Lane.

10 houses on Jury Close.

There are about 70-75 customers and each customer will be visited every fortnight.

You should be able to do 7-10 customers per day.

He knew where they all were and felt suited to the work. He knew he would have to speak to Dave about how much it would cost to take over the business but he of course would leave that until Saturday when he saw him.

Chapter Five.

A few days passed and Wilf did his usual cleaning and tidying of his small flat. It was a two-bedroomed place and it was cozy enough for him. He had a few different girlfriends over the years but never had time for a wife. He was quite content to look after himself.

He looked forward to Friday evening at the Grove. He would do all his washing and ironing and put on a smart pair of trousers, shirt, tie, and jacket. He liked his clothes and was very proud of his appearance. There would occasionally be a fancy dress party that he would go to. They had one at the Grove a few months ago and Wilf dressed as a cowboy. He had hired a cowboy suit and a stetson. He liked stetsons and when Rick went to America on holiday he brought him one back as a souvenir. Wilf cherished it and wore it on special occasions. He was very proud to own it and was quite a character when he was seen wearing it.

On Friday evening he arrived at the usual time. Smartly dressed and ready for the social evening. The other regulars arrived and they asked him about the business.

'How did it go Wilf?' they asked.

'Great.' he answered. 'We did some houses and businesses on Kings Drive and Queens Road.' 'I think I would like to take the business over but it depends on how much he wants for it.'

'That's true,' said Terry.

'It will be a few quid depending on how many customers there are and whether you think it will be worth taking on.' said Dale.

'Yes' said Wilf, 'We are going to have a chat about it tomorrow.'

'What the owner and you Wilf?' asked Don.

'Yes, I will see if we can come to some agreement tomorrow.'

'Good luck with that Wilf.' everyone responded.

They all raised their glasses and said,

'Here to Wilf and Beaton's Window Cleaning Business.' 'Have a drink on us!'

They all drank and laughed and the usual discussions took place.

Rick arrived a bit later that evening as he had been on a late shift.

He walked in bought a drink and sat down next to Wilf.

He said to Wilf,

'Hey, Wilf I have just walked in and there is a baby outside in a pram unattended.'

Wilf looked at him with a concerned face and said 'Hey, where?'

Terry overheard the conversation and said 'Hey, where?' too.

The three men walked outside and popped their heads around the corner. They saw a young woman sitting next to the pram with the baby in it. It looked as if the three guys were curiously looking at her.

When Wilf saw the young woman with the child he looked around and walked over.

Then he said,

'It's alright the taxi hasn't arrived yet!'

Terry and Rick looked at him and laughed. Then they all went back inside the pub.

'You idiot.' said Wilf. 'You told me there was no one with the child and I was only trying to help. It looked as if we were baby snatchers looking at that young mother with her child.'

Rick was trying to stop laughing but he replied,

'Wilf, it must have been a one-off. When I walked in here the lady must have just momentarily left the child and I thought it had been abandoned.'

'Yeah, your right' said Wilf but I had to think quickly and pretend that we were going outside to get in a taxi.

'Well, there is no harm done Wilf. I will go and speak to the lady if she is still there to explain what happened.'

'Alright if you wish.' replied Wilf.

Rick then went outside and the young mother was still there with her baby in the pram. He explained what had happened and she laughed. Rick said to the lady,

'It was just one of those one-off situations' he said.

The lady replied, 'I had just gone to my car to get the milk for the baby and I was only away for about 30 seconds as that is my car right there.' 'My husband is inside with his friends but I am not going in as I don't want the baby in a pub environment.'

'Ha, ha.' laughed Rick. 'Thank you it was nice talking to you.'

She replied, 'You too, your friend was really funny when he looked around and said it's not arrived yet!'

'Yes, he is a very caring person.' said Rick. 'Anyway, see you.'

With that, Rick returned and explained everything. What a funny mix-up.

They then had a few more drinks and the night went by. They departed at last orders and made their usual way home. Before they went Wilf had told everyone that he would take on the business as long as Dave and himself could agree.

Most of his friends were saying to him well it should be a fair business if the other guy had run it for several years. Don and Dale had said that they had seen Dave doing the windows for many years in the area. They did not know him but did know that he had been working as a window cleaner for a long time so the business must have been alright.

Wilf listened carefully to his friends' advice. He had worked most of his life and his flat was paid for so he knew that he could afford to take on the business. He also thought that if he did a good job the business would grow and develop.

'Just think Wilf if the business takes off you will have a Jaguar Car with your initials WB 1 on it with a set of ladders on the roof rack.' Terry said.

'Yes, Beaton's Executive Transparent Wall Technician Services, ha, ha.' replied Wilf.

Everyone wished him all the best with the meeting.' See you next week.' they said.

Chapter Six.

The following morning Wilf got up early and started getting ready for the day. He made his usual breakfast and then went out to meet Dave. He arrived at Dave Preston's at about 10.30 am.

He knocked at the door and Dave answered. They went inside and started talking about the business. After about a twenty minutes when Dave had explained who and where he could get water from on the round, where he could buy leathers, sponges, and window cleaning equipment at a cheap price, and which customers would pay immediately or at the weekend they talked about the fee for the business.

'Well, Wilf the business has served me for about 15 years. It is 1972 now and everything has gone up in price. It is a part-time job really but you could make it into a full-time one if you serve your customers well and work hard.'

Wilf sat back and thought for a minute then Dave and himself agreed on a fee for him to take the business over. They also agreed that Wilf would pay him the cash on Monday and Dave would give him a receipt and agreement to say that the business was now his. This would be given a stamp from a local lawyer, which Dave would pay for.

With that, they shook hands and Wilf took the business on. Wilf had also purchased the ladder and a bucket and took these out of Dave's lock-up garage. He had a shed at the back of his flat on Vineyard Street where he could put them.

He carried his equipment down the road and thought about his change of career. He saw a few people on his way home and let on to them.

'Window cleaning, Wilf.' one of his associates shouted.

'Yes, Beaton's Window Cleaning Service.' he replied.

Another person saw him and said, 'Good luck with your new adventure Wilf.'

'Cheers.' he replied.

Wilf arrived back at Vineyard Street and put his equipment in his shed and locked it up.

Dave had also given him another list with more details about the customers on the round and who would supply him with water if he needed it. Wilf had a look at the revised list.

Dear Wilf,

Here are a few more details.

10 houses on Moorgate Lane.

5 Businesses and 5 Houses on Kings Drive.

10 houses on Queens Road.

These places are next to each other. There is a water tank at the back of my house you can use for as long as I am here. You may have to make different arrangements when I have moved.

5 Businesses and 5 houses on Duke Lane.

These places are next door to each other and there is a water tank at the back of Mrs. Bishop's number 15 Duke Lane that I fill up once a fortnight. Mrs. Bishop will supply you with the water you need if it is empty.

<u>7 houses on Regent Drive.</u>

<u>7 houses on Royal Street.</u>

<u>8 houses on Court Road.</u>

There is a water tank at the back of 10 Royal Street which again I top up once a fortnight. Again these streets are next to each other.

<u>6 houses on Lawyers Lane.</u>

<u>10 houses on Jury Close.</u>

There is a water tank at the back of 1 Jury Close which gets topped up once a fortnight. Again the Lane and the Close are side by side.

My neighbour Mick comes out with me once a fortnight usually at the weekend and we fill up containers at the back of my house and go out in his van to fill up the other three tanks. It takes about an hour or so and he has agreed to carry on doing it for you if you like. He gets paid off me fortnightly and you can sort that out with him.

Most of these houses and businesses have been served by me for over 10 years and you may be able to get more customers if you wish as they will recommend you if you do a good job. Most of them don't mind if you ask them for water if you get stuck as you only visit them once a fortnight or once a month. In addition to the people, I have noted most people will cooperate as you will become part of their local community just like I have.

I input the tanks myself as the business developed and have always used them for the window cleaning service. I am sure you will be able to use them as I have done.

If you need any advice or help I will be here for a few more months yet and my door is always open. Good luck with it with Wilf and all the best with the business.

Dave Preston.

Wilf had not thought about the water situation that was one thing he had forgotten about. Nevertheless, Dave had explained a procedure that seemed to work and Wilf thought I will be able to turn my hand to this.

He went down to the hardware shop in the afternoon that Dave had told him to go to and bought a few more essential supplies for the business like new leathers, a new pair of overalls, and some window cleaning equipment.

He decided to stay in over the weekend as he was thinking about the week ahead. He looked at the list again and Dave told him to start at Queens Road and then do Dukes Lane as he had served most of the people on Moorgate Lane and Kings Drive the week before.

He advised Wilf to follow the list in chronological order as he had set out as this was when the customers would be expecting him. He also gave him a list of the numbers of each street that were customers so that Wilf knew which houses or businesses to go to. Dave had already informed most people that a new person would be taking over soon as he was retiring but had not told them who it was.

Chapter Seven.

The morning came on Monday 7th February 1972 and Wilf would start with his new career. He got up early and then got his ladder and equipment out. He took the ten-minute walk down Queens Road. The lightweight ladder was ideal for the job and he did not have any problems carrying it. It was one of the newest ladders out and he felt very privileged to be using it for his work.

He arrived at Queens Rd at 9.00 a.m. and took out the list Dave had given him. Numbers 1,3,5,7,9,17,18,19 and 20 Queens Road. Wilf then got some water from the nearby tank at Moorgate Lane and filled up his portable water container.

He then got started and was working very well. The weather was cold but it was dry and Wilf was doing alright. When he had finished number 1 he knocked at the door and a gentleman answered,

'Morning Sir, I am your new window cleaner, Wilf Beaton. I am replacing Dave.'

'Morning Wilf, let me have a look.' replied the customer.

The man walked into the garden and had a look at his windows.

'Very good, here's your money.' he said.

Wilf replied 'Thank you, I will be back in a fortnight and can do the inside of your house if you wish also.'

'I will think about it and let you know when you come back.'

'Great, see you in a fortnight.' Wilf replied.

He then moved to number 3 and when he was doing the back upstairs window the man who answered the door to him came out to have a look at his work.

'Come on,' he shouted. 'The windows are filthy and need a good cleaning.'

'Yes, I can see that.' he said. 'How did the windows get so dirty?'

'I had a barbecue here last week and the wind blew in and all the smoke from the cooker stained the windows.'

'Oh, I see.' said Wilf.

He started wiping and cleaning harder and the man watched him.

After a few minutes, he came down the ladder.

'There you are, Sir.' 'Nice clean windows.'

'Yes, here's your money.'

'Thank you.' said Wilf. ' I will be back in a fortnight and if you want me to do the inside of your house I can do them for you.' ' I know how to put window cleaner and polish on the inside of windows.'

'Fine' said the man. 'I will let you know in a fortnight.'

'Of course, it will be a little extra.'

'No problem' he replied.

With that Wilf moved on to the next house. He knew he was going to have to introduce himself and repeat himself quite a lot at the start. He reckoned that not many people were going to let him do the windows on the inside because he was new to the job and it would take time to build up trust. He thought that Dave must have done a lot inside as they knew him and it would take a little time for him to become accepted.

He finished the first few houses on Queens Road and then knocked at number 17 and a lady answered the door. His portable water container was empty and he asked if she would fill it up for him. The lady was very cooperative and did so. It was only a short walk back to Moorgate Lane but it saved him the journey.

'My name's Wilf Beaton and I have just taken over the business.'

'Nice to meet you, Wilf.' 'I am Mrs. Grennelly and Dave has been doing my windows for about the past ten years.' 'Are you going to do a good job for me?'

'Of course' he replied. With that he got to work and was leathering, cleaning, and singing.

'Oh, what a beautiful morning, oh, what a beautiful day, I've got a wonderful feeling everything's going my way.' 'The sky is as high as an elephant's eye.' Then he repeated the verse a few times as he did his work.

He finished the job, picked up his money, and said to Mrs. Grennelly that he would be back in a fortnight.

She thanked him for cleaning the windows and said he had done a good job and would tell one or two more people on the street about him if he kept up the good work. It was a built-up area and most people owned a car so the windows got dirty quickly and needed doing regularly. Wilf thought to himself that's great I am already building up a good rapport with the customers and hopefully will get some more. He thought to himself you know the old saying with every business if we please you tell others, if not tell us.

Wilf then finished the rest of the houses on Queens Road. He was lucky here as the street was made up of mostly pensioners and housewives who were at home so everyone had paid. He had some of the leaflets Dave had used in case anyone was absent and changed the script to put his name on it now.

By mid-afternoon, he had completed his work and started to walk back to Vineyard Street. Lightweight ladders, an empty water container, and a bucket were manageable for his walk home. However, the equipment was a little awkward walking down the pavement.

He had to be careful when he was crossing the road or turning corners. He always checked that nobody was immediately behind or in front of him when he walked around corners as he did not want to collide with anyone with his ladders. He again looked quite a character walking down the street with his overalls on and his leathers and sponges in his bucket. He had a few different hats to wear and thought about wearing his stetson for work but decided not to as that was just for special occasions.

He got home and put his equipment back in the shed. He went in and cooked some dinner. He was quite tired as he had not worked for a little while and it was taking a bit of getting used to climbing the ladders and walking for some time during the day.

He had a look at the list Dave had given him and realized that on the next day Tuesday he would be working on Duke Lane. There were a few businesses to do there so he would make a bit more money but he would have to put in more effort to make sure that the customers were satisfied. He thought about the next day and relaxed. Little did he know that the next day was going to be quite different.

Chapter Eight.

The next morning Wilf got up at the usual time. He made breakfast and rechecked his list. It was cold outside so he put a pullover on under this overall and made sure he had his hat on to keep him warm.

On Duke Lane there were 4 or 5 businesses one was an estate agent, another was a hairdresser, one was a flower shop, the next one was a greengrocer and the last one was a hardware shop. The remaining 5 houses on the street were numbers 2,4,8,10 and 15.

He took the usual walk down the road with his equipment. When he arrived at the estate agent's he introduced himself and filled up his water container and bucket there. He cleaned the outside first and then they asked him to clean the inside of the windows also. This was a place where customers came in and out so Wilf thought it would be easier for him to get more business here.

He realized that the estate agent was very clean and in nice condition.

The Manager Mr. Evans came out and Wilf introduced himself.

'Morning, Wilf Beaton your new window cleaner.'

'Morning, Wilf are you taking over from Dave?'

'Yes.'

'Great do the inside and the outside please?'

'Sure'

'How often are you going to come and clean the windows?'

'Every fortnight.'

'Fine.'

Wilf then said, 'It must be paying in here you have the shop in excellent condition.'

'We are doing alright thanks, Wilf. Here's your money.'

'Great.' he replied.

Wilf then moved on to the remaining businesses on Duke Lane. They all asked him to do the inside and the outside of the windows so it took a bit longer to complete. He worked well and picked up his money at each of them.

He was just about to walk back to Vineyard Street when suddenly the heavens opened. It started to pour down with rain. He waited inside the last shop which was a hardware store but it continued to bucket it down.

After about twenty minutes the rain stopped and Wilf went outside. He then picked up his ladder and equipment and walked briskly back to Vineyard Street. As he was returning it started lashing down with rain again and he got soaked wet through. It was still raining cats and dogs when he was putting his tools back in the shed and he ran into the flat.

He then ran straight into the bathroom and had a bath. He was quite tired but thought that he could still go out to meet everyone at the Grove later if he had a bit of tea and a rest beforehand.

After he had had a wash he got changed into his dressing gown and made himself a sandwich with a pot of tea. He put his overalls out to dry, got a different hat out of the cupboard, and put the other clothes he had been wearing on the radiator to dry. He remembered that it was Tuesday and Rick and Dale may turn up with their guitars and they could have a good old sing song later on. He thought to himself I will get changed later and have a quiet stroll out to the Grove at about eight o'clock.

He was watching the evening news at six o'clock and was looking forward to the night out. Being a bachelor can be lonely sometimes but it has its advantages and disadvantages like anything else. He was thinking about later on when suddenly the doorbell rang.

He didn't get many visitors and Wilf wondered who it could be. He got up a cautiously walked to the door and pulled it open answering the door in his nightgown.

Chapter Nine.

Two policemen in uniform stood at the doorway,

'Mr. Wilfred Beaton.' said one of them.

'Yes.' he replied.

'I am Detective Inspector Reeves C.I.D. Greater Manchester Police and this is Detective Constable Hilton.'

Wilf looked at them and was very surprised. He thought what are the Police doing here.

'We just have a routine inquiry and would like to ask you a few questions.'

' I know you were not expecting us, I can tell by the way you are dressed.' 'May we come in?'

'Sure.' said Wilf.

He let them in and they walked into the living room and sat down. Wilf then turned the television off and said,

'How can I help you?'

'I would just like to ask you Mr. Beaton can you remember where were you on 19th January?

Wilf sat back and said,

'The 19th January that was nearly three weeks ago. He looked at the calendar on the wall and then calculated twenty days I think to be precise. If you asked me where I was yesterday I would have to think about it.'

'Yes, I know, but can you remember?' asked Detective Constable Hilton.

'To be perfectly honest I can't remember.' said Wilf.

'Alright.' said Detective Inspector Reeves. 'If anything jogs your memory will you please contact me at Plough Lane, Police Station?'

'Certainly, I know where it is?' he replied.

'Fine, thank you Mr. Beaton and we are sorry for bothering you.' they replied.

'That's alright' said Wilf.

He then got up and showed them to the door they got into a car and drove away.

As soon as they had left it suddenly dawned on him that he had not asked them why they had called or explained what it was about. He realized that this was in the heat of the moment he had frozen because he was not expecting a visit from anyone, especially not the Police. He also thought they knew my name and knew where I live. They must have done some investigation to find these things out!

He felt the need to go out for a drink and got ready for his Tuesday evening at the Grove. As he was getting ready he was thinking about it. What happened? Why did they ask about where he was on a particular day? Something must have happened but he was unaware of it. He cast his mind back to his other job finishing and he was either at home, shopping, visiting Manchester, or had just returned from a short break in Bangor, North Wales.

What caused the Police to come round. They don't just call on people they call on people for good reasons. His mind was boggling a little but he began to think that it was just a routine inquiry and if he had done something they surely would have taken more action there and then.

Anyway, he got changed into his smart casual clothes and thought about meeting his friends at the Grove. It was Tuesday so they might be having a sing-song later and it would be a good way to relax. He thought about it and was thinking shall I say anything to anyone or just keep it quiet.

He thought a problem shared is a problem halved. But was this a problem? With that, he left the flat on Vineyard Lane and took the stroll down to the Grove. He arrived early bought himself a pint and sat down waiting for the other people to arrive. It was quiet for a Tuesday evening but he knew that the regular people would come. Rick had told him that he would be working in Newcastle the previous Tuesday evening for a few days but he would be back on Tuesday afternoon and maybe a little bit late arriving but would be there.

Chapter Ten.

At about 8.00 pm. the regulars arrived. Don and Terry walked in and sat with Wilf. Then Dale arrived a few minutes later. Don had been working with his Father and Terry had a temporary job at the local supermarket. He was having a year off and was planning to go to University later in the year. Dale had been doing his usual work and had been to night school for his guitar lesson.

They started chatting and Wilf told them what had happened earlier in the day. He was very surprised that the Police had turned up at his flat and was trying to figure out why they had come. Everyone listened to him and Terry said,

'It's probably just a routine inquiry, Wilf.' 'I was going home from here one night and I got stopped by the Police.'

'What happened' said Wilf.

'I left here and was running up the road when a Police car stopped and two coppers got out and said they wanted to have a word with me.'

'Yes, then.' Wilf replied.

'One of the coppers said to me.'

'Where have you been?'

I said 'I have been to the Grove.'

The copper said, 'Have you got proof of who you were with?'

I said ' Yes, I have been with some friends at the Grove.'

The other copper then said, 'You were running then weren't you?'

I said, 'Yes.'

He said, 'Why?'

I responded, 'I was just going home, that's all.' 'They didn't believe me and he got on his radio to the Police Station. I gave him my name and address and when he found that I had no criminal record he started thinking.' 'Next, a Police van came around the corner and four coppers got out from the back and surrounded me.'

'Were you afraid?' asked Wilf.

'No, I was quite confident because I knew I had not done anything and you should feel the same way, Wilf.'

'What happened next?' asked Wilf.

'The coppers got back in the van and left.' 'The initial two coppers asked me to come with them so I got in the car and they drove me down to a place not far from here.' 'One of them got out and the other one stayed in the car.' 'After about ten minutes the other copper came back and he said,

'I am sorry, we've made a mistake.'

I replied, 'What's wrong?'

He said, 'A guy has been breaking into houses in the area, you were on your own you fitted the description and you were running.' ' I thought it was you.'

'Ok,' I replied.

The copper then drove me to near my house and said,

'I will give you a lift but not drop you off at your house as it will look strange if your neighbours see you getting out of a police car.'

'Fine' I said.

We then drove back and the Policeman then apologized again. Before I got out of the car near where I lived he said,

'If you see this guy let me know!'

I said 'Fine.' 'I then got out of the car and walked home.' ' Then I thought to myself how the hell do I know who this guy is.' 'That was the end of it.'

With that Wilf felt a bit more relieved. He sat back and started to enjoy his beer.

Just then Rick walked in. He had just returned from Newcastle but had time to go home change and come out for the usual Tuesday evening. He didn't bring his guitar as he had been in a rush and had not been to night school that evening.

He sat with his group of friends and they told Rick Wilf's story. Rick then said,

'Put it to the back of your mind, Wilf.' 'It was just a routine inquiry.'

'They have got other things to be concerned about.'

'Yes' everyone responded.

Rick then said to Wilf

'Hey Wilf, I have been working in Newcastle for a few days and my son can't come to the match tomorrow night as he has got the measles.' 'I bought a couple of tickets for Manchester United v Newcastle United while I was up there.' 'Would you like to come?' 'You like football but you don't get the chance to go very often, it's alright you can have the other ticket as I am going.'

Wilf thought about it for a moment. He did not support any team really but with Manchester United being the nearest ground to home he used to go occasionally and wanted them to win when they played.

'Great' said Wilf. 'Where shall we meet?'

Rick said, ' I will pick you up at your apartment tomorrow at 6.30 pm.' 'The kick-off is at 8.00 pm.'

'Wonderful I am going to look forward to that. It has been ages since I last went to Old Trafford.'

'That's fine.' said Rick. 'I will pick you up then.'

With that Wilf felt even more relaxed. His friends had reassured him about things and he had something to look forward to free of charge.

Everyone carried on socializing for the evening and even though they did not have a sing-song they left feeling happy and content. They left at about 10.00 p.m. and everyone made their usual journey home.

Chapter Eleven.

Wilf got up on Wednesday morning and did his work. He was getting used to things already and cleaned the windows on Regent Drive. He filled up at the water tank at the back of 10 Royal Street.

He cleaned all seven houses on Regent Drive and most of the customers were in so he introduced himself and left a note at just a couple of the houses where nobody was around. He worked quite quickly as he was looking forward to the football match. He was finished in the afternoon and made his way back to Vineyard Street.

He washed, got changed, and had some dinner. He was watching the television and thinking about the other customers on the round over the next day or two.

He was ready to go out and at 6.30 pm the doorbell rang. He answered the door and not to his surprise this time it was Rick.

'Evening Wilf, ready to cheer on United?'

'Great, thanks for coming let's get over there.'

They jumped in the car and drove off to Old Trafford.

It took about half an hour to arrive and the streets and roads were very busy. Rick had been many times before and knew a place where he could park the car not far from the ground. He asked Wilf to pay for the parking because he was getting a free ticket so Wilf willingly paid for it.

They got out of the car and Rick gave Wilf his ticket and they walked to the ground. They queued up at the turnstile and went in. They then looked at the seat numbers and a steward show them to their places.

Suddenly, they realized that they had made a big mistake. Rick had bought the tickets in Newcastle so they were surrounded by Newcastle supporters. Wilf had brought his red Manchester United scarf and fortunately, it was winter so it was cold and he was able to hide the scarf down his coat.

The game kicked off and after about 20 minutes Manchester United scored.

Wilf put his hands together to clap and then suddenly realized where he was. He then put his hands down and said, 'Oh, no they've scored.' To his great relief, nothing happened and he was a bag of nerves as his scarf fell out from under his coat as he went to applaud.

The first half ended and Wilf looked at Rick and said, 'Come on I'm going home.' Rick whispered, 'It's alright just keep quiet.'

The second half started and Manchester United got a second goal and then a third. Wilf was motionless and he could see all his friends celebrating at the other end of the ground.

There were about ten minutes left and people were leaving. Wilf said to Rick, 'Let's go now.' Rick whispered in his ear, 'It's alright United might get another goal.' During the last few minutes, Manchester United scored a fourth goal and the Newcastle fans started going crazy and were ripping the seats out of the stadium.

To Wilf's great relief the game ended but things were not over yet. When they got outside the stadium they had to start running to get away from everybody else. They ran and both men were out of condition when they got to their car they were completely out of breath and exhausted.

By some miracle, they had
managed to survive the game
without getting harmed and Rick
drove Wilf back to his flat. When
they arrived back it was quite late
and Wilf said to Rick, 'Do you
know something, Rick?' 'What's

that Wilf.' he replied. 'That will be the last football match you will ever see me at.' Rick didn't say anything he just watched Wilf get out of the car and make his way into the flat.

Wilf then made himself a cup of tea and sat down shaking. He thought that his life was becoming rather adventurous. He thought of the Police last night and a dangerous football match tonight. Will anything happen next?

Chapter Twelve.

Thursday morning came and Wilf arose again. The next job to do was the seven houses on Royal Street. He was becoming more familiar with the work now and was getting the hang of it. He started a little bit later in the morning and the weather was cool but dry so he did not have any problems.

He filled up his water container again when he had finished three of the houses. The semi-detached houses on his round had the usual bay window at the front, two upstairs windows, two or three windows at the side, and four windows at the rear.

When he had finished in the afternoon he took what was becoming the usual walk back to

Vineyard Street. He was thinking about shopping at the weekend but had enough food in to keep himself going until then. He was already becoming quite a familiar character and the work seemed to be suiting him.

He got home, had a wash, and changed. He cooked dinner and then watched the television. He looked at the list Dave had given him and realized that the next day he would be working at the eight houses on Court Road.

The next day was a typical one or so he thought getting everything ready, walking, cleaning, leathering, filling up his water container, collecting money off the customers, and leaving a note for anyone who wasn't in. Most of the people on the round were retired so he picked up most of the money on the way and made a note of the people who were not in so he could call on them the following week.

He again arrived back at Vineyard Street and got ready for the usual Friday night out. He had had an unusual week, the Police calling on Tuesday and going to the football match on Wednesday. The last two days had been normal and that's how he expected things to go.

He got changed again into his smart casual clothes and walked down to the Grove. He bought a pint and sat down in the same place waiting for the others regulars to arrive. A few minutes later Freda Jenkins the landlady of the pub came over to Wilf and said,

'Good evening, Wilf how are you?'

Wilf replied, 'Fine thanks, and you?'

'Fine. By the way, a Policeman has been in here this afternoon asking me about you.'

At that moment Wilf was drinking his beer and he suddenly choked and spat some of it out.

'What.' he replied.

'Yeah, a Detective has been in here and he was asking questions about you.'

'What was his name?' he asked.

'Detective Constable Hilton.' she answered.

'What was he asking?' asked Wilf.

'How long had we known you and had you been buying people more drinks than what you usually did?'

'What did you say?' he asked.

'I told them that I had known you for as long as I had run this pub since 1965 and that you were a nice guy and we had never seen you in any trouble.' 'I also said that you had not been flamboyant with money recently and that you had not been buying people more drinks than what you usually did.' Freda explained.

'What exactly is going on?' said Wilf. 'He came to my flat the other day with an Inspector and they were asking where I was on January 19th. That was nearly a month ago and I cannot remember.' ' Why have they been coming in here and asking about me?'

'That explains it' said Freda.

'Explains what?' asked Wilf.

'Did you not hear about the robbery on Kings Drive, Wilf?'

'I don't know what you are talking about?'

'There was a robbery and a load of money and valuables got stolen at one of the houses on Kings Drive. It was in the local paper and it happened a few weeks ago.' 'They

must be carrying out inquiries.'
'Everyone has been talking about it.'

'Except me, that must be why they were asking you had I been buying more drinks' said Wilf.

'Yes. Like I said Wilf I told them I had known you a long time and they asked me did I think you would do something like this.?'

'Oh, that's alright.' replied Wilf.

'You are alright I told them that I don't think you've had anything to do with it.!'

'What!' Wilf choked and said,

'You told them you didn't think I had anything to do with it!'

'Yes.' she replied.

'Oh no, that has got them thinking now. You should have said don't be stupid he wouldn't do anything like that.' 'They will go away now thinking.'

'Well, sorry Wilf I only did what I thought was right.' said Freda.

'You've got me thinking now.' said Wilf.

With that Freda got up and went back behind the bar. She started serving customers with the rest of the bar staff and looked over at Wilf from time to time.

His other friends then arrived Don, Terry, Rick, and Dale. Rick said to Wilf, 'Alright mate.' 'Do you want to go to a football match?'

Wilf sarcastically looked at him and then told everyone about what Freda had just told him.

Terry said, 'Hey, Wilf when I got stopped it was a few weeks ago. Maybe it was the same day but I can't remember now.' Then Dale said, 'Well, they seem to be interested in you Wilf. They will be inviting you down to the Police Station next.'

'Hey.' said Wilf. 'This is not funny. It is playing on my mind now they have been to the flat and now they have been in here asking questions about me. I am getting worried about this.'

Rick tried to reassure Wilf by saying, 'Look, Wilf, these things happen. Look at the football match we were in the wrong place at the wrong time.' 'This has been in the local press and everyone knows what it is about.' 'All of us here will testify for you to say that you would not do anything like this.' Freda added.

Are we all agreed on that?' Rick asked everyone. Everyone nodded.

'Hang on.' said Wilf. 'The Police have not been to see any of you and they seem to be more interested' in prosecuting me than leaving me alone.'

'Listen again.' said Dale. 'Everyone has heard and read about the robbery on Kings Drive in the local paper.' 'Everything will be okay.' 'This has been in the local press and everybody knows what it is about.'

'You have got tied up in this in some way or form. If the Police come here again we will tell them that you are a nice, caring person and that you would never do anything like this.' 'You have been a law-abiding citizen for as long as we have known you and this is something that you wouldn't do.'

'Thanks for your help and concern.' said Wilf.

With that, the social evening continued but it was noticeable that Wilf was finding it more difficult to relax, and trying to put this to bed was easier said than done. He was thinking about where he was. Was he in North Wales? Was he at home? He was in between jobs he was pretty sure about that. Who can tell the Police of my whereabouts if they ask?

Chapter Thirteen.

The following day Wilf awoke and got himself ready for the day. He did not work at weekends and the job was only really a part-time thing. He needed a bit of money to tide himself over. He had been a bachelor all his life and had worked for a couple of companies and saved some money along the way. He wasn't rich but he had enough to keep everything going and that was all he was particularly interested in.

He made a list of what he needed in the way of shopping from the local supermarket and checked his fridge and kitchen to see what was in and what wasn't. He wrote out the list as he was watching the television and when he had checked everything he put his coat on and made sure he had his bank card with him to get some money from the ATM.

He had changed his shopping day to Saturday as he was working on Fridays now. He turned the television off and made his way to the front door. Suddenly, the doorbell rang. He was on his way out so he answered and once again the two policemen were standing at the door, Reeves, and Hilton.

'Morning Sir' said, Detective Inspector Reeves.

'Morning.' Wilf replied. 'Look what exactly is going on you came here on Tuesday and now you are here again.' 'I have heard that there was a robbery on Kings Drive a few weeks ago.' 'Is this what this is about?' he asked.

'Yes.' said Detective Constable Hilton. 'It is an inquiry into that and well……...

Sir, do you mind coming down to the Police Station with us please?'

'What for?' asked Wilf.

'We would like to take your fingerprints.' said Detective Inspector Reeves.

Wilf then stared at both of them with a worried look on his face and said, 'Alright you will have to hang on a minute as I was about to go shopping and I will have to put the bags I was going to use back in the kitchen.'

'Fine' they said. 'We will wait in the car outside and take you down to Plough Lane when you come out.'

Wilf was then sweating a little and getting very concerned. Lots of things were running through his mind.

Will they take me to the Police Station and lock me up?

Will, I have to give a statement after I have given my fingerprints.?

Will they start to interrogate me at the Police Station?

Will they start asking me more questions?

All these things were starting to run through his mind.

He came out of the flat, locked the door, and got into the car. They drove down to the Police Station and went inside. They then gave him a document and he gave his fingerprints. They then left the room and left him there on his own for about ten minutes. Wilf was thinking long and hard and then they returned.

'Fine, we can give you a lift back to your flat if you wish?' said Inspector Reeves.

'Thank you.' said Wilf. 'You mean I am free to go now?'

'Sure.' the Inspector replied.'Detective Constable Hilton will give you a lift home.'

'Fine.' said Wilf. They then left and gave Wilf a ride back to his flat.

When they arrived he got out and went in to pick up his shopping bags. All sorts of things were now playing on his mind. He went out to catch the bus to the local shopping centre and felt the need to have a pint because of the pressure he was under. He caught the bus and went into a pub first for a couple of pints. He then went shopping and picked up the usual things that he needed for the week.

When he had finished shopping he got a taxi home and was getting rather paranoid.

He was thinking to himself what if I get home and they are waiting for me again?

What sort of things are they going to ask? What shall I say?

Who told them about me? I am a suspect.

All these things were racing through his mind and he was trying to weigh up what if anything would happen next.

Chapter Fourteen.

On Sunday, February 13th Wilf was thinking about the situation. He was wondering if Dave Preston would have known anything about this. After all, this happened when Dave still had the business and if he knew anything why didn't he say anything to him. After an uneasy night's sleep, Wilf decided to go and visit Dave to see if he could find anything out.

He arrived at Dave's house on Moorgate Lane in the middle of the morning. Wilf knocked and waited and Dave answered 'Good morning, Wilf how are you?

'I am not too good actually can I come in and speak to you please?'

'Sure' replied Dave and they then went inside to the Living Room.

Wilf explained to Dave everything that had happened over the last few days and then he asked, 'Did you know anything about the robbery on Kings Drive?' 'Sure.' Dave replied. 'It was all over the local press a few weeks ago.'

'Yes, they came here a day or two after it happened. I wasn't doing the window cleaning that week, I was doing a bit of Truck Driving in Manchester.'

'What did the Police do?' asked Wilf.

'They went to see the agency I was working for and they verified that I had been working for them that day and for the few days after the robbery happened on...........'

'January 19th' Wilf interrupted.

'How do you know that Wilf?' Dave asked.

'I have been having bad dreams about it. The Police have been asking about me in the Grove and have been to my flat twice asking where I was on that day.

'Really.' said Dave. He thought for a moment and then said.

What I think has happened Wilf is that somebody has seen you cleaning the windows in the area and they have rang the Police Station up and said there is a guy who works in that area as a window cleaner.' 'Window Cleaners work on their own a lot and you have not got an alibi.'

'Dave, I think you are right. I know we have not known each other for very long but I think what you are saying is true. They are suspicious of the fact that they don't know where I was on the day of the robbery.'

'Right' said Dave. 'They could be on the brink of arresting you on suspicion of robbery or whatever the crime was.'

'Yes, I think that too now.' said Wilf.

'Well, there is only one thing for it Wilf.' 'You are going to have to remember where you were.'

'Hmm, that is not going to be easy.' he replied. 'This was a few weeks ago now.'

'They could come around again Wilf and this is going to put you in the hot seat.'

'I know.' 'Well, I better start thinking about this in case that happens.' he replied.

'Not being funny, Wilf I am just being realistic.' 'They could come at any time and may want you to do some explaining.' said Dave.

'True' Wilf replied.

With that Wilf and Dave shook hands and he took the walk back to Vineyard Street slowly and thoughtfully. He was trying to weigh up what was going to happen next. He was now getting paranoid and on his way home and saw a Police car driving down the road. He thought oh no they are going to stop and start asking me more questions. Thankfully, this did not happen but he was finding himself constantly looking over his shoulder and was thinking that they might turn up again at his flat or when he returned they would be waiting for him.

All sorts of things were going through his mind and he could not rest or gain any sort of peace of mind.

When he arrived back at the flat he sat back and thought about everything. He was getting even more paranoid as there was a programme on the television about somebody who had just been released from prison for being falsely accused of a crime. He quickly turned the television over and started trying to think of other things.

It was becoming more difficult to relax and Wilf was so worried about the situation.

Chapter Fifteen.

On Monday morning February 14th Wilf headed for Lawyers Lane. There were six houses to do and he was going to leave the next street on Jury Close to do on Tuesday and Wednesday. During, the rest of the week he was going to revisit the houses where the people were not in initially. When he had finished those he was going to start on Moorgate Lane and carry on in chronological order from the list Dave had given him.

He was trying to keep the law and order issue to the back of his mind but this was impossible to do. He found himself looking over his shoulder all the time and lived in the fear that the Police would reappear at any moment. He managed the six houses in good time during the morning and early afternoon. By the middle of the day he was finished and again he took his usual stroll home.

He turned into Vineyard Street, put his equipment away and went inside. He looked out the window and to his horror, the Police were there again. This time it was not Reeves and Hilton but two other uniformed officers. Wilf was nearly shaking with what he saw and what made it more embarrassing was that the neighbours could see the Police outside his flat.

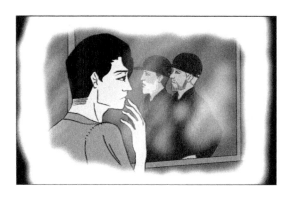

He slowly opened his front door.

'Mr. Beaton' said one of the officers.

'Yeah' he replied.

'I am P.C. James Morgan and this is P.C. Paul Brown.'

'G-G-Good evening.' Wilf stuttered.

'We just have a routine inquiry.' P.C. Brown said.

'Where were you on January 19th this year?'

Wilf stopped and thought for a moment. He had thought about this already and reckoned that he was in North Wales on the day of the robbery. He then looked at both of them and replied in a shallow quiet voice,

'Well, I think….'

Then P.C. Morgan shouted 'WHAT DO YOU MEAN YOU THINK?'

'Well, I was in Bangor, North Wales on January 19th to the best of my knowledge.'

'I was in between jobs and went there for a break.'

'Where did you stay?' asked P.C. Brown.

'I stayed at the Seaview, Bed and Breakfast in Bangor and the people who own the place are called Mr. and Mrs. Checker.'

'How long did you stay there for?' P.C. Brown asked.

'About a week as I was brought up there during the war and went back on a visit.'

He then gave them the full address of the place where he told them he had stayed and as they left they said to Wilf.

'This better be correct and you better be telling the truth.' said P.C. Brown.

'It is.' said Wilf rather softly. 'As far as I can remember that is where I was.'

With that, they drove away and Wilf was staring into space.

Lots of things were now going through his mind and he only hoped that he remembered the correct date for when he was away as he had not kept the train ticket but was sure that the Police would contact the B and B to check that he was there on that particular day.

He was pretty sure that he was away then? Would this be his alibi?

However, he was also thinking what if the date wasn't correct?

Surely, they would come back and accuse him of lying.

Would the Police return and say that they did not believe him?

What would happen then? Who had given the Police the information about him?

Did he have the right to ask how did they find out about him?

Would they return take him to the Police Station and detain him?

Chapter Sixteen.

Tuesday morning came and Wilf got things ready for work. He walked down the main road and towards Jury Close. There were 10 houses to do but his anxiety had taken over his thoughts and he decided to just do half the street and then return. He was trying to take his mind off things but was constantly looking over his shoulder worrying that the Police would turn up.

He did his usual work cleaning and filling up and was trying to think about the Tuesday evening social at the Grove. He worked until about dinner time and then took the walk back to Vineyard Street. He spent the afternoon cleaning and tidying the flat and getting ready for the evening but his nerves were getting the better of him.

He did his afternoon jobs followed by getting himself ready for the usual Tuesday evening social at the Grove. He left the flat at the same time and took the walk down to the local town. When he entered the Grove, he bought his drink and sat down. Freda and Mick, the landlady and landlord were behind the bar and Freda waved at him. Wilf walked over and said.

'Good evening, Freda, have they been back in here asking about me again?'

'No' said Freda.

'But there is time yet.' said Mick jokingly.

'Hey, stop pulling my leg Mick, this isn't funny.' replied Wilf.

Just then his other friends Don, Terry, Rick, and Dale arrived.

'Evening Wilf.' said Don. 'You're still free!'

'Yeah, I thought we would have been coming to visit you.' joked Terry.

'Stop going on about this, you know how worried I am.'

'Yes, stop it fellas.' said Dale. 'This has got past a joke now.' he exclaimed.

His friends then tried to give him some reassurance. They stated how this was probably just a routine inquiry. With every case, there was a list of suspects and the Police had to go around and get an alibi for the group of people they suspected of committing the crime.

Dale tried reassuring him further by saying, 'Look, Wilf, if they thought you would have done this surely they would have arrested you by now and took you in for questioning.'

'They have already done this except arresting and detaining me!' he replied.

'Well sure, they would have put you in for one of those identification parades if they thought you were a front-line suspect.' said Rick.

'Hey, I haven't thought about that.' Wilf replied. 'They could still do that.' 'They have been to my flat and they have been in here asking Freda all about me.'

'You're joking.' said Rick.

'No, it's true, they were asking had I been buying people more drinks than I usually did and then they asked her did she think I would do something like this.? 'You know what she then told the Police?' everyone remained silent and looked at him.

'You're alright, I told them that I don't think you've had anything to do with it.'

Everyone stared at Wilf.

'That wasn't the best thing to say was it?' said Wilf.

'No, if anything it will get the Police thinking.' said Don.

'Quite right.' he replied.

'If I were you I would look into challenging them for harassment. They have been to your home, they have been in here and it is causing you all sorts of headaches.' said Terry.

'Your right.' 'This surely can't go on it is driving me mad.' said Wilf.

With that, they carried on with the social evening as best they could. Wilf was still in an uneasy state as he was thinking all the time about what if anything would happen next and wasn't making jokes about it anymore. This was something that he never imagined in his wildest dreams would ever happen but in some way or another, he had got caught up in a Police investigation about a robbery.

What would happen next everyone thought?

Chapter Seventeen.

On Wednesday morning Wilf awoke and got ready for the day. He had the remaining houses to do on Jury Close. He got everything ready and took his walk down to the place. His mind was in a tense state but he got on with his work to try and take his mind off it.

He finished the houses just after lunch and then saw that he was running short of some cleaning equipment. He put his equipment back in his shed and took a bus to go to the place where Dave had told him he could get cheap cleaning equipment for his work.

He bought a few things and then took the bus back to Vineyard Street. He was thinking about the people who were absent when he called and looked at the list Dave had given him. He had ticked off the houses and businesses he had cleaned and started making a fresh list of the houses he needed to revisit. He thought this would be a good way to finish the week and restart at Moorgate Lane next week.

When he got home, he sat down and turned the television on. After he had had dinner he started to look at the items he had bought for the window cleaning. New leathers, sponges, cleaning liquid, and a window wipe. Dave did know where to buy things at a discounted rate as he was very surprised about how reasonable the prices were in the shop.

At about six o'clock there was a knock at the door. Oh no, Wilf thought to himself. He had tried to take his mind off things and this was bringing everything back. Is this the Police again? If it is what am I going to say? What are they going to say? Will they take me to the Station and charge me? What will they do?

He slowly and cautiously walked and answered the door.

To his great relief it was Terry. 'Good evening, Wilf! How are you?'

'Relieved, I thought you were the Police coming to arrest me.'

'Yes, they have come to me asking about you now and……………..'

Wilf interrupted and said 'WHAT!'

'Wilf I am joking.'

'Phew.' 'Here don't wind me up again like this you know how I feel.'

'Wilf I have come to help you.' Terry replied.

'How?' said Wilf.

'Let's have a cup of tea and I will show you.' he said.

They then went inside and Wilf put the kettle on and made some tea. He brought the tea and biscuits in and sat down with Terry. Terry then pulled out a copy of the Salford Evening News. He flicked through the paper and said.

'Bear with me a second Wilf I am just trying to find it.'

Wilf waited patiently.

'Here we are Wilf.' 'Have a read of this.' and he gave the newspaper to Wilf. The headline on the page read,

YOUTH ARRESTED ON SUSPICION OF THEFT.

A 16-year-old youth from Manchester who cannot be named for legal reasons has been arrested on suspicion of theft. The youth was found asleep on Deansgate in Manchester city centre this morning. He was picked up by the Police and found to have expensive rings, bracelets, and necklaces that have been linked to robberies in the Salford area. Further Police investigations are ongoing.

'Well.' said Wilf. 'I just hope that this is right and the Police have caught the right person.'

'So do I.' replied Terry. He then said,

'It looks to me as if this person broke into places including the one on Kings Drive a few weeks ago stole money and valuables and the Police have now found him asleep on the street.' 'To me, he has probably used all the money he stole on staying in places and when his money ran out has been back on the street.' 'I think it would have been difficult for him to sell the valuables because he is a young down and out and if he went to a jeweller's or a pawnbroker's trying to exchange them for cash no one would trust him or want to do business with him.'

'Terry, I hope you are right.' 'Surely, if they link the valuables to the house that got robbed on the round, that is it and this bad dream should end.'

Chapter Eighteen.

The next morning Wilf had a look at the revised list that he had made out. There were about 12 places to revisit and he was hoping to get around all of them by the end of the day. He was having to visit nearly every street on the round but they were all close to each other so he reckoned he could revisit and do most of the work by the evening. His plan of action then was to restart at Moorgate Lane and Kings Drive next week.

Most of the people were in and he did his usual filling up where necessary and introducing himself to the people who had not been in when he first called. He was thinking of the Friday night at the Grove and what had happened the previous evening had given him a bit more peace of mind. He was finishing on Jury Close as a couple of people had not been in on his previous visit. He introduced himself, did his work, and then picked up the payment.

It had been a long day and he was quite tired. He had put the equipment away got washed and changed and was going out for a walk to try and clear his head. He was walking back towards Vineyard Street in the early evening when suddenly a car pulled up beside him. His heart was racing like a moped as he thought it was the plain clothes police. Then, he realized it was Terry again in his car.

'Evening, Wilf.' he said.

'Phew! Alright, Terry. God! I thought you were the Police.' Wilf replied.

'Here I will give you a lift home.'

'I have just finished work and have something else to show you.'

With that, Wilf got in the back of the car. As they were driving back to Vineyard Street, Terry gave Wilf a copy of the Salford Evening News.

'Turn to page 10 Wilf' Terry said.

As they drove back Wilf started reading the article. The youth had been charged with theft. Some of the valuables had been linked to the robbery in the area. Some of the banknotes had been linked and spent at some shops and other places in the vicinity.

The youth had previous convictions for theft and shoplifting. He had also been seen at some of the places he robbed as some witnesses had testified that it was him in an identification parade. His fingerprints had also been found at the crime scenes so it looked as if the nightmare was over.

Wilf then looked at Terry and stared around with a sigh of relief.

'Thanks for this Terry.' he said.

'I don't usually buy a newspaper but I will keep buying one now until this person is dealt with.' ' If you had not come along this could well be playing on my mind.' 'I appreciate your concern, Terry.'

'Not at all.' Terry replied. 'What are friends for?'

They then arrived back at Vineyard Street and Terry opened the car door for Wilf.

'Coming in for a coffee?' asked Wilf.

'Love to but I have got to get the dinner ready tonight as my folks are away and the rest of the family are working late, so I promised them I would get something ready for them when they come in.'

'Ok, are you going to the Grove tomorrow night?' asked Wilf.

'Sure, look forward to seeing you there.' said Terry.

'I owe you a drink.' said Wilf.

'No problem.' 'See you tomorrow night.'

With that, they shook hands and Terry drove off. Wilf in a bit more of a relaxed state walked in with the best peace of mind he had had for nearly two weeks.

Chapter Nineteen.

The next day was Friday 18th February 1972 and there were about 6 or 7 places on the round that Wilf had not cleaned as the people were not in. He thought I will revisit these today and finish early. Despite, the fact that he had been given great reassurance he was still concerned and when a Police car passed him by on the street and drove on he was quite relieved.

Only a couple of the people were absent so he did about half a day's work. He did his usual work cleaning, leathering, drying, and in some cases polishing. He was thinking about the Grove in the evening and what people would say but the interrogation thoughts had not left him yet. He cracked on with his work and got things finished quite quickly so he was home just after lunchtime.

He was starting to have second thoughts about the window cleaning. After all, it was winter and the weather would be nicer in the summer time. However, in the autumn and winter, the nights would be cold and dark and he did not think he would like the work then. He also reckoned that he might be better getting another cards in a job where he went to work and picked up this money at the end of the week. He would not have to worry about paying his tax or his national insurance stamp then either. He also knew that he would not have to buy new equipment even though it wasn't very expensive and if he was ill or sick a company would pay him.

He was thinking about this as he was getting ready for the Friday night drink at the Grove. What would Dave think if he said he did not want the window cleaning round now? That didn't matter. He could sell it to somebody else if he was going to pack the job in. He wondered about these things and then went down to the Grove.

When he arrived Terry, Dale, Don, and Rick were already there and they cheered as Wilf walked in.

'Well, you are still free!' said Don.

'Yes, they haven't locked you up yet.' joked Rick and everyone laughed.

Wilf looked at them with a very serious face. Then he said,

'Stop going on about this.' 'I am still not over it yet and alright the Police haven't come to me for a few days now but you never know what might happen.'

All his friends said that they had seen the report in the newspaper. They all felt quite confident that the Police had found the culprit and that he was just in the wrong place at the wrong time.

Wilf had been so confused and upset that he had forgotten to tell them about what the Police had asked him on Monday evening which was the last time they called at his flat. He explained that he thought he was on holiday in Bangor, North Wales and that the Police had probably contacted the place where he stayed the Seaview Hotel which was run by Mr. and Mrs. Checker.

'Hey, Wilf you didn't tell us about that on Tuesday.' said Rick.

'No, I forgot because my mind was all over the place.' he replied.

'That's it then.' 'They would have contacted those people and eliminated you as a suspect because they said that you were there on January 19th.' said Terry.

'I hope so, I just had a bit of doubt whether I was there or not then as I had not kept the train ticket and could not remember what exact dates I was there from and to..' Wilf replied.

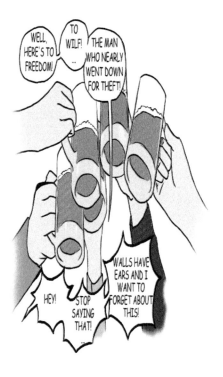

'Well here's to freedom.' said Dale as everyone raised their glasses.

'To Wilf, the man who very nearly went down for theft.' said Don.

'Hey, stop saying that walls have ears and I want to forget about this.' said Wilf.

'Yes, the last two weeks of your new year and a new career, Wilf sure have been different.' 'After all visits by the Police, the Police asking about you in here a trip to the Police Station, and a dodgy football match all within the first two weeks of becoming a window cleaner.' said Rick.

'What's going to happen next?' said Freda and Mick Jenkins the landlord and landlady of the pub who had overheard the conversation.

'Hey.?' 'They haven't been back in here have they?' asked Wilf.

'No.' 'Sorry, Wilf we weren't being nosy but they had read the paper and were so happy to read that somebody has been charged with the offence.'' I know we did not say exactly the right thing to them but we all hope that justice has been done now.'

'As well as that Wilf a Mr. and Mrs. Checker telephoned here today and said that you had left your diary at their hotel and that they had just found it.'

'You are not on the phone but our contact details were in it. They found it in your room and telephoned and said that you had stayed with them for seven days from January 15th to January 22nd as you had written this in your new diary for the year and it corresponded with their visitors' book records.' 'They said they would send it on to you but wanted to check that your address was correct as it was written in the diary.'

'Thank God for that.' said Wilf. 'That is further proof that you thought,

I DID NOT HAVE ANYTHING TO DO WITH IT!'

Everyone then laughed and began to enjoy the evening. Wilf had a few beers with his friends and started to become his usual self again.

Wilf did think about whether or not the Police had contacted Mr. and Mrs. Checker and thought about telephoning them to find out. However, after a while, he thought no it would look a bit strange if I rang them and asked had the Police been in touch about me. Even if they had he now had further evidence of his innocence for something that he did not do.

Chapter Twenty.

Over the weekend Wilf started to think long and hard about the window cleaning round and thought that he would be better off working for somebody else. Although he was suited to the work it had made him a bit paranoid and apprehensive as he did not want anyone to have the fortnight he had just had.

He went to see Dave Preston on Sunday afternoon and again had a long conversation with him in his living room. He explained about the horrendous fortnight he had just experienced and Dave was interested to hear about it.

'Dave, I have been thinking.' said Wilf. 'This has been a bit of a misadventure for me.' ' I like the work but the experience has been rather unique and I feel that a change of work environment is what I need.'

Dave listened carefully to Wilf and said,

'You weren't the only person interested in the window cleaning round Wilf.' 'Two or three other people came forward and I may not be retiring down to Cornwall for a little while yet as things are not as ready down there as I thought they would be.' 'I am building a house there to retire to with my wife but the planning permission is taking longer than I thought it would and it is looking like next year before we can go.' said Dave.

'I will rebuy the business off you for the same price as we agreed before and resell it to somebody else soon.' 'Like I said two or three other people were interested and it won't take long to show them what to do.' 'After all, it is only a part-time position and would suit somebody who is semi-retired which the other people are.'

With that, they shook hands and Wilf agreed to give Dave the ladders and equipment back. He went to his shed that afternoon and returned the work tools to Dave's lock-up on Moorgate Lane.

When he returned Dave said to him,

'I can get Mick my neighbour who fills up the tanks to do the round for as long as it takes to get somebody else. He has just been made redundant and will welcome the job for a week or two as he has done it for me before when I have been on holiday.'

'Great mission accomplished.' said Wilf.

With that Wilf returned to Vineyard Street. He saw a few children playing in the street and it was a quiet Sunday afternoon. He wondered about what would be his next job and was quietly confident that he would secure something locally in a factory or maybe as a school caretaker or something like that. He didn't need much money at the moment as he had money saved, so he wasn't in a hurry to find another job and knew he would get something eventually. There was one thing for sure he wouldn't be working as a window cleaner again.

He stopped outside his flat and found a cleaning cloth in his pocket. He thought this will be a nice souvenir of his two-week adventure as a window cleaner. There was one thing for sure although it had been a real difference it wasn't a nice thing to happen and he will remember it as a nightmare.

He was going to have another break at home for a week or two and then start looking for another job. He was looking forward to Tuesday evening and could not wait so he decided to dress in his smart casual clothes and go down to the Grove this evening.

He put on his stetson and cowboy boots and walked in wearing his jeans and a casual shirt. When he walked in Freda and Mick saw him and said,

'Hey, Wilf have you found a new career as an actor?' They asked.

'Anything considered' he replied 'except being a window cleaner.'

' A pint please.'

With that Wilf in his cowboy
outfit danced to his favourite song
with the locals playing music in
the background while he sang,

'I am a rambler, I am rambler from Manchester way I spend all my money the hard working way. I maybe a workman on Mondays, but I am a freeman on Sundays. Ha, ha.

Printed in Great Britain
by Amazon

83624189R00108